Farmyard Tales Flip Books

Pig gets Stuck

Heather Amery

Illustrated by Stephen Cartwright

Language consultant: Betty Root
Series editor: Jenny Tyler

There is a little yellow duck to find on every page.

This is Apple Tree Farm.

This is Mrs. Boot, the farmer. She has two children, called Poppy and Sam, and a dog called Rusty.

On the farm there are six pigs.

The pigs live in a pen with a little house.
The smallest pig is called Curly.

It is time for breakfast.

Mrs. Boot gives the pigs their breakfast.
But Curly is so small, he does not get any.

Curly is hungry.

He looks for something else to eat in the pen.
Then he finds a little gap under the wire.

Curly is out.

He squeezes through the gap under the wire.
He is out in the farmyard.

He meets lots of other animals in the farmyard.
Which breakfast would he like to eat?

Curly wants the hens' breakfast.

He thinks the hens' breakfast looks good.
He squeezes through the gap in the fence.

Curly tries it.

The hens' food is so good, he gobbles it all up.
The hens are not pleased.

Mrs. Boot sees Curly.

Curly hears Mrs. Boot shouting at him.
"What are you doing in the hen run, Curly?"

He runs to the fence.

He tries to squeeze through the gap. But he has eaten so much breakfast, he is too fat.

Curly is stuck.

Curly pushes and pushes but he can't move.
He is stuck in the fence.

They all push.

Mrs. Boot, Poppy and Sam all push Curly.
He squeals and squeals. His sides hurt.

Curly is out.

Then with a grunt, Curly pops through the fence.
"He's out, he's out," shouts Sam.

He is safe now.

Mrs. Boot picks up Curly. "Poor little pig," she says. And she carries him back to the pig pen.

Curly is happy.

"Tomorrow you shall have lots of breakfast," she says. And Curly was never, ever hungry again.

Patch runs back to them.

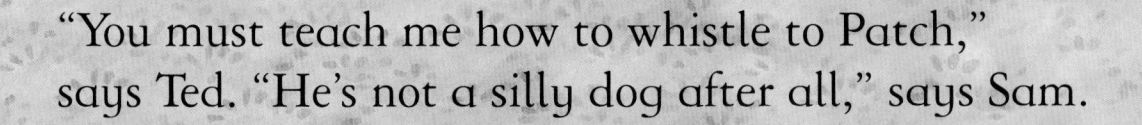

"You must teach me how to whistle to Patch,"
says Ted. "He's not a silly dog after all," says Sam.

Ted stares in surprise.

"Patch doesn't do anything I tell him," says Ted.
"You don't know how to whistle," says the boy.

The boy whistles to Patch.

Patch chases Woolly back through the gate.
She runs into the field with the other sheep.

The boy has found a sheep.

"There's Woolly," says Sam. "I found her on the road," says the boy. "I was bringing her back."

Patch has found a boy.

The boy pats Patch. "Hello," he says. "I wondered who bought you when my dad sold his farm."

Patch dives through the hedge.

Patch barks and barks. "What has he found?"
says Sam. They all go to look.

"Where's Patch going?" says Sam.

Patch runs away across the field. Ted, Sam, Poppy and Rusty run after him.

They go to the sheep field.

"Look," says Sam. "One sheep is missing." "Yes, it's that naughty Woolly again," says Ted.

Sam shouts at Patch.

"Come here, you silly thing. You're meant to be
a sheepdog. Ted will have to send you back."

Then they look at the pigs.

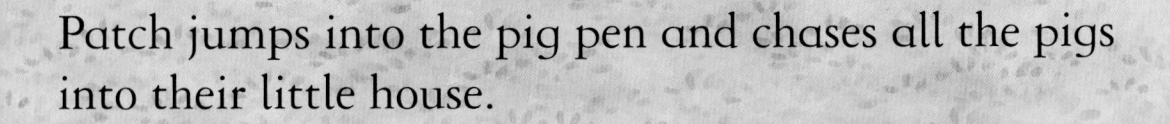

Patch jumps into the pig pen and chases all the pigs
into their little house.

"Now we'll go and see the cows."

Patch runs into the field and barks at the cows.
But they just stand and stare at him.

First they look at the hens.

Patch jumps into the hen run and chases the hens.
They are frightened and fly up onto their house.

Poppy, Sam and Rusty say hello to Patch.

"Come on, Patch," says Sam. "We'll show you all the animals on our farm."

Ted works on Apple Tree Farm.

He has just bought a sheepdog to help him with
the sheep. The sheepdog is called Patch.

This is Apple Tree Farm.

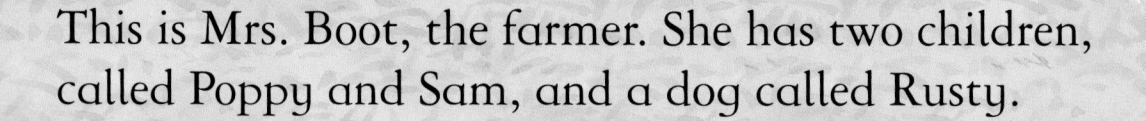

This is Mrs. Boot, the farmer. She has two children, called Poppy and Sam, and a dog called Rusty.

Farmyard Tales Flip Books
The Silly Sheepdog

Heather Amery

Illustrated by Stephen Cartwright

Language consultant: Betty Root
Series editor: Jenny Tyler

There is a little yellow duck to find on every page.